# Little Shaq
## Star of the Week

**Books by Shaquille O'Neal and
illustrated by Theodore Taylor III**

*Little Shaq*
*Little Shaq Takes a Chance*
*Little Shaq: Star of the Week*

# Little Shaq
## Star of the Week

## SHAQUILLE O'NEAL

illustrated by
Theodore Taylor III

BLOOMSBURY
NEW YORK  LONDON  OXFORD  NEW DELHI  SYDNEY

To Dale Brown and the Buss family
—Shaquille

To my son, Theo. I'm sure I'll be
reading this to you soon.
—Theodore

First published in the United States of America in October 2016 by Bloomsbury Children's Books
Paperback edition published in October 2017
www.bloomsbury.com

Bloomsbury is a registered trademark of Bloomsbury Publishing Plc

Shaquille O'Neal™; Rights of Publicity and Persona Rights: ABG-Shaq, LLC. shaq.com

For information about permission to reproduce selections from this book, write to
Permissions, Bloomsbury Children's Books, 1385 Broadway, New York, New York 10018
Bloomsbury books may be purchased for business or promotional use. For information on bulk purchases
please contact Macmillan Corporate and Premium Sales Department at specialmarkets@macmillan.com

The Library of Congress has cataloged the hardcover edition as follows:
Names: O'Neal, Shaquille. | Taylor, Theodore, III, illustrator.
Title: Little Shaq : star of the week / by Shaquille O'Neal ;
illustrated by Theodore Taylor III.
Description: New York : Bloomsbury, [2016]
Summary: Little Shaq has always wanted his own kitten, but his parents aren't sure he is responsible
enough. When Little Shaq is chosen as his class's Star of the Week, he's sure it's his moment to prove
that his parents can count on him. Will Little Shaq be able to show he's ready for his very own pet?
Identifiers: LCCN 2015047031 (print) • LCCN 2016010115 (e-book)
ISBN 978-1-61963-879-2 (hardcover)
ISBN 978-1-61963-880-8 (e-book) • ISBN 978-1-61963-881-5 (e-PDF)
Subjects: LCSH: O'Neal, Shaquille—Childhood and youth—Fiction. CYAC: O'Neal, Shaquille—Childhood
and youth—Fiction. Responsibility—Fiction. | Pets—Fiction. | African Americans—Fiction. BISAC:
JUVENILE FICTION / Readers / Chapter Books. JUVENILE FICTION / Sports & Recreation / Basketball.
| JUVENILE FICTION / Social Issues / Friendship. | JUVENILE FICTION / Family / Parents.
Classification: LCC PZ7.O549 Lk 2015 (print) • LCC PZ7.O549 (e-book) | DDC [Fic]—dc23
LC record available at http://lccn.loc.gov/2015047031

ISBN 978-1-61963-882-2 (paperback)

Art created digitally • Typeset in Chaparral, Housearama Kingpin, and Shag Expert Lounge
Book design by John Candell
Printed in China by C&C Offset Printing Co., Ltd., Shenzhen, Guangdong
1 3 5 7 9 10 8 6 4 2

All papers used by Bloomsbury Publishing, Inc., are natural, recyclable products
made from wood grown in well-managed forests. The manufacturing processes
conform to the environmental regulations of the country of origin.

# Table of Contents

# Chapter 1
# MVP

Little Shaq couldn't wait for school to start. His teacher Ms. Terpenny would announce the next Star of the Week any minute.

"I think it's going to be Aubrey," said his neighbor Rosa Lindy.

"I bet it's Barry," said Aubrey Skipple.

"Really?" asked Little Shaq's cousin Barry.

Little Shaq didn't know who Ms. Terpenny was going to choose, but he hoped it would finally be his own turn.

"Quiet, everyone. Walter needs to take attendance," said Ms. Terpenny.

Walter was Aubrey's twin brother and the current Star of the Week. Walter had lots of responsibilities, like taking attendance and passing out the snacks at break time. And last weekend, he looked after Flopsy, the class rabbit.

Little Shaq loved Flopsy, but she wasn't his favorite part of Star of the Week. Tomorrow was Walter's last day as the star, and he would get to do Show and Tell. Little Shaq thought Show and Tell

was the best thing ever. He'd been
making a list of what he'd bring
in since the beginning of the year.
There was his seashell collection
from the Jersey Shore, a photo of his
family at Nana Ruth's birthday party,
and his very special autographed
basketball from the All-Star Game.

When Walter finished taking
attendance, he took his seat next to
Little Shaq.

"Well done, Walter. You've been

such a bright star this week," said

Ms. Terpenny.

Little Shaq patted his

friend on the back.

"And now," Ms.

Terpenny continued,

"it's time to announce the next Star
of the Week."

Little Shaq felt his tummy tighten.
He crossed his fingers underneath
his desk.

"The next star has a passion for
learning . . . ," said Ms. Terpenny.

Little Shaq
smiled. He loved
school. His
favorite subject
was history.

"This student always lends a helping hand . . . ," Ms. Terpenny went on.

*Mom says that I'm a great helper*, Little Shaq thought.

"And this student is a leader in the classroom *and* on the basketball court," Ms. Terpenny concluded.

Little Shaq's eyes grew wide.

His teacher had a big smile on her face. "Our next Star of the Week is Little Shaq!"

The class erupted in cheers and applause.

Ms. Terpenny handed Little Shaq a certificate and instructions for him to share with his parents. It was

official. Little Shaq was Star of the Week!

After school let out, Little Shaq and his friends walked to the rec center to play basketball.

"You're going to be a great Star of the Week," said Rosa.

"Totally! Being Star of the Week is like being the MVP of a basketball game," said Walter. "And you're really good at that."

"Thanks!" said Little Shaq, but he suddenly felt nervous.

Being the MVP was a tough job. Coach Mackins taught him that it took problem solving, teamwork, and practice to be successful.

"Hey, look at this!" said Aubrey. She was pointing at a flier on the rec

Parkview Elementary
PET FAIR

Mon.-Fri. Afternoons
Rec Center

Find the perfect pet
for your family!

center's front door. "There's going to be a pet fair here all next week!"

"No way!" said Little Shaq. "You guys are so lucky that you already have pets."

Walter and Aubrey nodded. They had a brown, furry dog named

Monty. Rosa's cat was Mittens, and

Barry had a tropical fish

named Louie.

"Maybe you could

bring your parents to the

rec center," said Barry. "I bet the fair

will have kittens."

Little Shaq had been asking for a kitten for as long as he could remember.

"I don't know," he replied. "They've never said yes before."

That night during dinner, Little Shaq was nervous about bringing up the pet fair to his parents. He was so nervous that he couldn't even eat his favorite meal. His spaghetti and meatballs sat on his plate untouched, but his parents didn't notice. His

younger brother, Tater, had made
a tower out of meatballs that had
fallen over in a saucy mess. Mom

was not happy. And his older sister,
Malia, was going on and on about
her school play. Finally, Dad caught
Little Shaq's eye.

"How was your game today,

buddy?" Dad asked.

"It was okay," he answered. "We

lost, but the rec center is having a

really cool event next week."

"Oh yeah?" asked Mom.

Little Shaq took a deep breath. "Yeah, they're hosting a pet adoption fair."

"Shaquille, we've been through this before," said Mom.

"A pet is a lot of responsibility," said Dad.

"I *am* responsible!" said Little Shaq.

"What about your chores?" asked Mom. "We always have to remind you to make your bed."

Little Shaq sighed. It was true. He wasn't good at remembering to take out the trash, and Mom did have to tell him every morning to make his bed. He couldn't understand the point of making it, if he was just going to get back in it later.

Little Shaq shook his head. There had to be a way he could prove he was ready for a kitten before the fair was over. He glanced around the

room and saw his backpack. His Star
of the Week instruction sheet was
sticking out from the top.

In all the excitement about the
pet fair, Little Shaq had forgotten to

tell his parents the big news. "Wait, starting Monday, I'm going to be Star of the Week," he said. "I'll have loads of responsibilities!"

"That's true," said Malia. "Being Star of the Week is a lot of work."

"Yeah," piped in Tater, even though he was way too young to know.

"Plus, I have to take care of Flopsy this weekend," Little Shaq added. He grabbed the instruction sheet and handed it to Mom. "If everything goes well, *then* can I get a kitten?"

Mom and Dad looked at each other and laughed.

"We'll think about it," they said.

Little Shaq smiled.

It was a start.

# Chapter 2
# TATER'S TURNOVER

At the end of school the next day, Walter was finishing up his Show and Tell. He had already shared his soccer trophy, his favorite book, and his clarinet.

"And last, but not least, this is my grandpa's marble collection," he said. "He gave it to me for my birthday."

Walter held up a box with multicolored marbles. "Gramps says he lost a few, but I counted, and they're all there."

The whole class clapped as the bell rang.

On Monday, Little Shaq would be Star of the Week, but his first job was to watch Flopsy over the weekend.

"Are you coming with us to the rec center today?" Barry asked Little Shaq.

Little Shaq frowned. "I can't. There's no one to watch Flopsy while I play, so my mom is picking us up."

"Aw man, I was hoping you'd try to dunk," said Barry.

"Me too," Little Shaq replied. He

didn't want to miss the game, but he knew that being responsible meant he couldn't always do what he wanted.

After his friends left, Little Shaq and Ms. Terpenny took Flopsy outside and waited for Mom to arrive. Ms. Terpenny went over Flopsy's instructions one more time: give her fresh water every day, line her cage with clean newspaper, and feed her in the morning.

Little Shaq sighed. Flopsy sounded

like a lot of work. So far, being Star of the Week wasn't so great.

Soon Mom pulled up, and once they were home, Little Shaq placed Flopsy's cage in the family room. Tater followed close behind.

"Watch out, Tater!" Little Shaq shouted. "Stop putting your fingers in her cage."

"But she's so fluffy," said Tater. "Can I pet her?"

"All right," said Little Shaq.

"But first we need to change her newspaper and give her fresh water. Do you want to help?"

"Okay," said Tater.

Little Shaq handed him Flopsy's water bottle. "Can you refill this at the sink?"

Tater took the bottle and ran into the kitchen. Then Little Shaq grabbed a sheet of newspaper to line Flopsy's cage.

"Come on, girl," he said, opening her door. Flopsy hopped forward, and he carefully picked her up just like Ms. Terpenny had showed him. With his free hand he rolled up the old newspaper and then slid the new one in. Flopsy felt warm and soft in the crook of his arm. Little Shaq smiled. Flopsy was pretty fun after all.

"Here you go," Tater said, handing Little Shaq the water bottle.

"Thanks," he said. "You can pet her now, but just lightly on the head."

"Can I feed her a snack?" Tater asked.

Little Shaq gave him a handful of lettuce. "Don't let her nibble you though," he said, tickling his brother under the arm. Tater giggled.

When Flopsy had finished eating, Little Shaq cleaned up and put her back in the cage.

"But I wanted to play with her," Tater whined.

"She needs to rest," Little Shaq said. "I'm going to shoot some hoops in the driveway. Want to come?"

"No!" Tater yelled and ran out of the room.

Outside, Little Shaq tried to forget about Tater being mad and the game he was missing at the rec center. He dribbled the basketball back and forth and shot a few layups, but he really wanted to dunk the ball. He'd been trying to dunk for the past few weeks, but he kept falling short. Coach Mackins said that in a few years he might be tall enough to do it. Little Shaq thought he'd try again anyway.

He backed up to the end of his driveway then took off running. He dribbled the ball toward the basket

and leaped into the air, raising his
hands high. He was almost there!
Little Shaq reached for the rim, but
then—

"Shaquille! Where are you?" Mom yelled. She sounded mad.

"Huh?" Little Shaq twisted his body toward the house and his dunk fell short. He landed hard on the ground and the ball rolled into the bushes.

Little Shaq shook his head then went inside. "What's up?" he asked.

"Flopsy is gone," Tater squeaked.

"Gone?" Little Shaq shouted. "She was in her cage!"

Tater hid behind Mom's legs. "I wanted to play with her."

Little Shaq's stomach sank. If he lost Flopsy, there was no way he could still be Star of the Week. He'd miss Show and Tell, and he could forget about going to the pet fair too.

"Mom, this is all Tater's fault!" Little Shaq cried.

"Tater was wrong," Mom said, giving her younger son a stern look. "But Flopsy is your responsibility. You need to find that rabbit and clean up this mess."

Little Shaq looked around the family room and saw a trail of destruction. There were shredded newspapers,

chewed slippers, and tiny brown

pellets everywhere.

"Okay, Tater," Little Shaq said,

"you look under the sofa in here and I'll take the kitchen."

In the kitchen, Little Shaq opened cabinets and searched the pantry, but Flopsy was nowhere to be found. She wasn't in the family room either.

Upstairs, Little Shaq and Tater each searched their rooms. Mom said hers was all clear. The last one to check was Malia's.

Little Shaq knew he wasn't supposed to go into his sister's

room, but this was an emergency. He

peeked inside. Flopsy had definitely

been there. He was about to search

Malia's closet when he spotted

Flopsy on the bed. She looked just

like one of Malia's stuffed animals. Little Shaq let out a sigh of relief.

Having a pet was tougher than he thought, but once Flopsy was safe and sound, Little Shaq got the hang of it.

For the next two days, he followed all of Ms. Terpenny's instructions and Tater even helped out too. By the end of the weekend, Little Shaq was ready to be Star of the Week.

On Monday morning, Little Shaq's

first job was to take attendance. He didn't think it would be too hard,

but standing at the front of the room, he suddenly froze. Little Shaq gripped Ms. Terpenny's clipboard and stared out at his classmates. He couldn't speak! Ms. Terpenny nodded for him to begin. Little Shaq gulped then read the first name on the list: Douglas Alvarez. No one responded, and Little Shaq felt his cheeks get hot.

Doug was sitting at his desk, chatting with his neighbor.

Little Shaq checked his name off the list and tried the next person, but this time he spoke too fast.

"You need to speak slowly and loudly," said Ms. Terpenny.

Little Shaq nodded okay. After a few more minutes, he finished the list, but he wasn't looking forward to doing it again tomorrow.

Later that afternoon, it was time for Little Shaq to pass out the snacks.

"Go get 'em," said Rosa.

"Yeah," said Barry. "By the way, I'll have the pretzels and save me an apple juice too."

Walter laughed and gave Little Shaq a thumbs-up.

Little Shaq picked up the snack

basket and started at the back of the
room. The first few rows were really
easy. Something was finally going
right!

"I'll have the pretzels, please," said Suzy Carmichael.

Little Shaq looked in the basket. There was only one bag left.

"Oh, see, these are for Barry," he replied.

"You can't save snacks," said Suzy. "Ms. Terpenny!"

"Fine," he said. "The pretzels are all yours."

Barry and Little Shaq both wound up with carrot sticks and skim milk.

While Barry grumpily ate his snack, Little Shaq left his untouched. He wasn't hungry. He just wanted the day to be over.

# Chapter 3
# BUZZER BEATER

As the week went on, Little Shaq tried his best to be a good star, but he wasn't getting better. After another slow start with attendance, Little Shaq thought about what Walter had said. Being Star of the Week was a lot like being the MVP. He knew that MVPs were problem solvers, and he was good at that on the court. He could do this too.

Suddenly, Little Shaq remembered the voice of his favorite basketball announcer. It was loud and clear, and it always got his attention. If Little Shaq could sound like him, his class might listen.

Little Shaq cleared his throat. "Douglas Alvarez!" he said in his best announcer voice.

Doug responded right away.

Little Shaq tried the voice again.

"Suzy Carmichael!"

"Here!" said Suzy.

It was working! Now he wondered if he could fix the snack problem too.

Little Shaq had paid attention to the number of students who asked for each

55

snack. If he brought a list to Mrs. Stewart, the lunch lady, she could fill the basket with the snacks that made his class happy. This would require teamwork, but he hoped Mrs. Stewart would agree.

During recess, Little Shaq went inside to the cafeteria. Mrs. Stewart was at the counter setting out a bowl of apples.

"What can I do for you?" she asked.

Little Shaq explained his plan and gave Mrs. Stewart a list with all the snacks he needed.

SNACK LIST
5 carrots
9 pretzels
6 apples
6 milk
7 apple juice
7 orange juice

"What a good idea!" said Mrs. Stewart. "You're a very responsible young man."

The next morning, Little Shaq made his bed without being told. He was getting better at that too. Practice makes perfect, his mom always said.

Mom and Dad seemed happy, and at school, Ms. Terpenny was impressed after attendance.

"You've made quite an

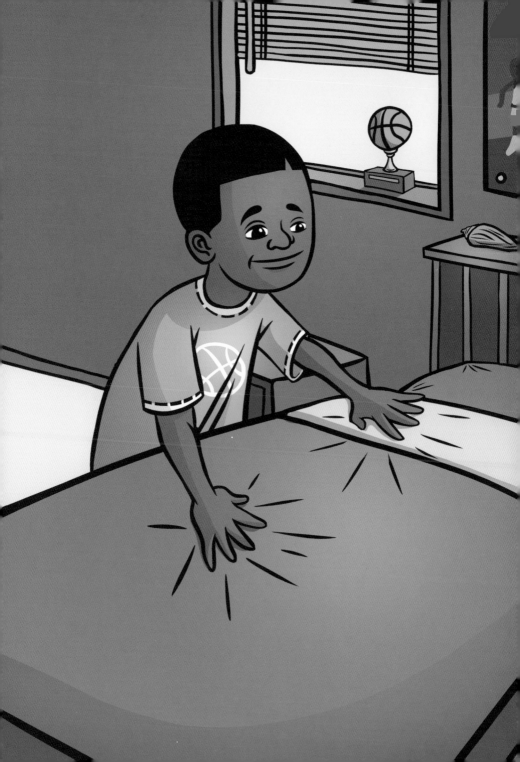

improvement," she said. "You should be very proud."

"Thanks, Ms. Terpenny," said Little Shaq. "I am."

Later that day, Little Shaq went to the rec center to play basketball.

Coach Mackins blew his whistle and Barry dribbled the ball down the court, bouncing it from hand to hand.

Little Shaq quickly got open and Barry passed him the ball. He wanted to go in for the dunk, but

he knew he wasn't ready. Instead,

Little Shaq lined up for the perfect

fadeaway jump shot.

He heard chants of MVP coming from the stands filled with his classmates, but when he looked up, he saw his whole family cheering too.

After the game ended, Little Shaq met them at the bench.

"What are you doing here?" he asked.

"I seem to remember there's a pet fair going on," said Mom.

"Really?" Little Shaq jumped up and down.

"We're only here to look," said
Dad.

Little Shaq, Barry, Malia, and
Tater sprinted over to the fair.

While everyone else looked at the

Labrador puppies, Little Shaq kept walking. At the end of the next row, he found what he wanted. Asleep inside a crate was an orange kitten with black stripes. It reminded him of a tiger, his favorite kind of cat.

Little Shaq reached in and carefully lifted the kitten. He cradled it in his arms, knowing that this was his cat. When he looked up, Mom and Dad were behind him.

"Can I get him?" he asked.

Mom glanced at Dad. "Let's take the night to think about it."

The next day Little Shaq took attendance and passed out snacks for the last time as Star of the

Week. On Monday, it would be Barry's turn.

In the final hour of school, Little Shaq set up his table for Show and Tell. He waved to his family in the back of the room. He noticed a cardboard box at Tater's feet that was probably filled with toys to keep him busy.

"Before we start with Show and Tell," said Ms. Terpenny, "let's give a round of applause to our Star of the Week!"

The whole room clapped.

Little Shaq felt his cheeks get hot, but he wasn't nervous this time. He said thank you and started his presentation. His seashell collection and the photo from Nana Ruth's party were big hits, but his All-Star basketball blew everyone away. Little

Shaq passed it around so his class could see the signatures.

When the basketball returned to Little Shaq, he began to pack up his things.

"Wait!" Tater yelled just as the bell was about to ring. "You've got one more thing!"

Dad reached into the box. Tater clapped his hands with excitement.

"We thought you could tell your class about this guy," Dad said.

Little Shaq couldn't believe it. Dad was holding the kitten Little Shaq had picked out at the fair! He gave Dad a big hug and scooped up his new pet.

"Everyone," said Little Shaq, "this is my cat, Tiger!"

That evening, Little Shaq watched TV with his brother, sister, and brand-new kitten. He was so happy he even let Tater watch his favorite show about lizards. After a few minutes, Tiger hopped down from the sofa and left the room. At the next commercial, Little Shaq followed.

But when Little Shaq walked out,

he saw something strange. A roll of toilet paper was streaming from the bathroom. He ran over to pick it up, but Mom was already there. Tiger was shredding toilet paper all over the floor. Mom turned to Little Shaq and raised an eyebrow.

Little Shaq just laughed. "Don't worry, Mom. I've got it!"

**Shaquille O'Neal** is the author of the Little Shaq series, a retired basketball legend, a businessman, and an analyst on the Emmy award–winning show *Inside the NBA* on TNT. During his nineteen-year NBA career, O'Neal was a four-time NBA champion, a three-time Finals MVP, and a fifteen-time All-Star, and he was named the 1993 Rookie of the Year. Since his rookie year, he has been an ambassador for the Boys & Girls Clubs of America, a group with which his relationship goes back to his youth in New Jersey. Passionate about education, O'Neal earned his undergraduate degree from LSU, his MBA from University of Phoenix, and a PhD from Barry University.

www.shaq.com
@Shaq

**Theodore Taylor III** is the illustrator of the Little Shaq series and was awarded the Coretta Scott King/John Steptoe New Talent Award for his first picture book, *When the Beat Was Born*. An artist, a designer, and a photographer, Taylor received his BFA from Virginia Commonwealth University and lives in Washington, DC, with his wife and son.

www.theodore3.com